The Ta

A Life Remembered

By

Margaret Eubanks

Worn, patched and frayed, the Tattered Bag has taken many journeys. It holds precious memorabilia of a woman's travels, keepsakes, and secrets, known only to her.

A medical diagnosis reveals that death is near. Unwilling to tell her family, having them watch her die was out of the question.

She decides to take one final journey with her beloved dog, Frank, and the Tattered Bag.

Laughter and sadness would fill her final days, and happiness would fill her last breath.

Dedication

This book is dedicated to my Mother, Ruby. I love you.

I've always loved you, Mom
And in my heart you'll stay.
When times seemed so impossible,
You never walked away.
You held your head so high,
Though you struggled every day.
The one thing you always said,
That God would make a way.
If only I had done more,
To help you in every way.
God, kept his word and so did you,
You're the reason I'm me today.
No one will ever take your place,
No one will ever be.
As precious in my life,
As you have been to me.

Cover Art by Chad "Viking" VanStory

Index

Chapter 1
A Good Day-Gone Bad

"What does it matter what day it is?" Margaret thought. "I'm retired."

All that's important is today-the warm sunshine on my face, a hot cup of coffee, and relaxing out on my screened-in porch with Frank, my dog, and planning our day of adventure.

Every day of the last five years since my retirement has been wonderful. Today was my anniversary date of my last day at work, and my memories took me back.

How good it felt to punch that time clock for the last time after thirty years of service at age fifty-one.

My feet would thank me; no more steel-toed shoes, safety glasses, or ear plugs. However, I would miss the smell of fresh beer, but not the taste of that vending machine coffee!

That was the perfect place to work being twenty one years old. Everyone that worked there called it the biggest beer joint in town. Free beer in the break room, but always in moderation.

Saying good-bye to friends and co-workers was hard. I spent more time in that brick and mortar than at home. Memories made it difficult to take that final walk. Would I be remembered?

There was no need for a schedule anymore. My life was mine and it could change daily. I intended on taking it day by day, but I did want to spend more time with my family.

Andrew was a senior in high school and a baseball player. Even though, I couldn't go to all of his games I went to many of them. He was becoming a fine young man. My hope was that he would go to college, but I would support his career choice whatever it was.

Luke was three years old and ready to take on the world. I wanted to take him places and teach him things.

Then there was Frank, my adopted dog. He was so calm and laid back that he was a joy to have around. When I got him, he had been whipped, shot and left to die.

I was looking forward to all of these challenges. Thirty years of unfinished projects and new ones to come. I'm not going to rush myself, I'll plan for tomorrow another day.

I went to the kitchen for another cup of coffee and the phone rang. I answered it without looking at the caller I-D, and all I remember was the word, "Cancer."

Oh, my God, not me, not now! My doctor wanted to schedule some test as soon as possible. We made the appointment, and I hung up the phone.

I screamed, I cried, I prayed. I tried to compose myself, however, I went numb. How could I tell my family? I wouldn't. Not now.

Two days later, I had the test and awaited the results. Four days later the results shook my world. There was no cure, for this cancer, only drugs to prolong my life. I had three to six months, maybe.

I needed to live longer. There are so many things to do. Who would be a grandmother to Andrew and Luke? Who would take care of Frank? I needed them, and they needed me.

All I could think about was death. I was unwilling to put this burden on my family. I would put this disease in God's hands, and make the best use of the time I had left.

Would my family forgive me, or understand my decision to do this my way? I couldn't bring myself to say good-bye. My heart was breaking, and I was prepared to lie knowing what telling the truth would do.

I cried into my pillow. We are slipping away from each other, I realize with sweet sadness and longing. This is the most horrifying episode in my life.

I was devastated and there was no escape. My life was in crisis, a living hell. It was almost over. This moment, this heartbeat, this breath, everything is not ok. This is the worst day.

Life is so unpredictable, yet so precious. Sometimes our plan doesn't work out, and right now is all we have. My choices are few.

I want to cry and scream, though I am far from giving up. I am not in denial, I am angry and acceptance comes hard.

There is no bargaining. It must be total surrender to God, but never giving up hope. Death can never take my spirit.

Following my dreams hasn't always been easy. Sometimes life throws us a curve ball we can't avoid. Early in life, I made a decision to go after my dreams. They took me in a direction unknown, but my journey was worth it.

In the most difficult of circumstances I must live each day. Soon my old life will be gone forever. What remains on my to-do list? Who will keep my family going?

I pray tonight, "Make me thankful that I am not anyone else."

****

I need to gather my thoughts and get my affairs in order. I am searching for a way to be thankful for all I have had. A trip would be perfect; Frank and I would go on a journey. There was money in the bank, and I had a new car. Perfect timing.

I packed a few suitcases, got two coolers from the storage shed, and pulled the old tattered bag from the back of my closet. Although it was old and worn, it served a great purpose.

The tattered bag contained secrets of a hidden life, memorabilia of my family, and hopes of peace that these memories would bring during this difficult time in my life. This would be the tattered bag's last journey.

I loaded the car, closed up the house, and last of all, loaded my dog, Frank. As we backed down the driveway, tears ran down my face. One last look for me to remember.

My red azalea bushes in full bloom, two redbud trees blooming a soft lilac color. My flower beds filled with every color of impatiens and huge bunches of hosta as their back drop.

Most impressive of all was the "Yard Of The Month" sign. Years of hard work had paid off, and I was so proud. I looked at Frank knowing that our life would never be the same again.

South, yes, Frank, I think we'll go south!

Chapter 2
The Starfish

Frank was a great traveling companion because he loved to ride in the car. After a few bathroom stops and two hundred miles, I found a roadside park so we pulled off for lunch.

The park was small, about the size of a baseball diamond. There were eight picnic tables and lots of shade trees. As we walked around, Frank sniffed and marked everything!

I got a sandwich and drink from the cooler. Then I fixed Frank a bowl of water and some snacks. After lunch, we got back in our car and continued our journey.

Later that day, we pulled off the interstate and got a room at the Holiday Inn. We checked in and went to the room. It had been a long day, and we were ready for supper.

There was a restaurant next door, so I went and got us a plate, and after we ate, we took our final walk. It began to get dark, so we headed back to the room.

When we turned the corner, Frank spotted the swimming pool. I knew how much he loved the water, so I broke the rules and let him take a swim.

Finally, we got back to the room, got our baths and prepared to settle down for the night. We climbed in bed, and Frank laid across my feet.

I called my daughter and told her about our first day. Andrew was on a date, and Luke was watching a Harry Potter movie. I told her that I would call her in a few days. We said our good-nights and hung up the phone.

I prepared to take my regiment of medicine wishing it could save my life, but knowing it was simply buying me some time.

I reached for the tattered bag, opened it and pulled out a white napkin. Inside was a delicate treasure, a starfish, no bigger than a dime. I found it while walking on the beach at Paradise Island in the Bahamas.

I brought it back home and added it to my shell collection. I displayed all my shells in an aquarium with sand and no water.

When Andrew started walking, he found the aquarium and soon discovered the starfish. He would point at the starfish and say, "Dis, I want dis!" I would take the starfish out and put it in his hand. He smiled and carried it all around the house.

We thought he would break it, but he never did. When he was ready to go home, he would hand me the starfish, and I would put it back. I made sure it was in the same place, so he could find it when he came back.

I put the starfish back in the napkin and gently placed it in the tattered bag. Then I whispered, "I love you, Andrew."

Frank wanted to go outside, so I put him on his leash, and off we went. He marked almost every tire in the parking lot. When we got back, it was a snack for him and a cigarette for me.

Then it was lights out. What a wonderful day!

Chapter 3
The Red Coin Purse

I woke up early and took Frank for a short morning walk. We stopped at the lobby, and I got a cup of coffee then we went back to the room.

We decided to check out the town. It had many old buildings in need of repair and beside the courthouse was a small park. I hooked Frank up, and we began our adventure.

All of a sudden, Frank spotted a squirrel and the chase was on. I had sixteen feet of retractable leash to catch up with them. The only thing that saved me and the squirrel was a huge oak tree.

After I caught my breath, we walked back to the car. I got out a blanket, the small cooler and found a shade tree perfect for a break.

A bowl of water and a munchy bone hit the spot for Frank. I lit a cigarette, opened my coke and sat on the blanket beside him. He decided to take a nap, and I was ready for the peace and quiet.

I spotted a man in the distance. He was leaning against a tree with his backpack beside him on the ground. He looked at us. All I could think was don't come over here! Too late, he was walking toward us.

He was unshaven and scruffy looking. His clothes were wrinkled, and he walked with a limp. The closer he got, I realized that his shoes didn't match and one of them was missing a heel.

He said, "Hello! Could you spare a coke and cigarette?"

I replied, "Sure."

He sat down, and we began to talk. He rubbed Frank's head and introduced himself. His name was Galaspy. He was a long way from home and just wanted to make a friend, something he had very few of.

The sad story of his life touched my heart. He was born and raised in Mississippi. His family was poor and survived on other people's handouts.

His family lived in a shack back up in the woods. Several days a week he would hitch the mules to his wagon, and go house to house picking up anything people were throwing away.

"Surely, there must be a better way of life than that." I thought.

He told of his travels during the night . This way he could avoid the excessive heat during the day. He asked me to watch his backpack while he went to the restroom to clean up.

"Once before," he said. "While I was in the restroom, someone tried to steal my things, and they beat me up!"

While he was gone, I reached in my pocket, pulled out a twenty dollar bill and put it in his backpack.

He came back, thanked me for my kindness and walked away. When he looked back, I waived and wished him well. He smiled and that made my day. I realized that I had misjudged him because of his circumstances. I met a friend today, and he met a fool!

I folded the blanket, grabbed the cooler, got Frank hooked up and headed back to the car. Up ahead on the right was a pond. I knew better than to take him up there, but what the hell!

The closer we got, the harder he pulled. All of a sudden, there were ducks everywhere! Oh shit! Oh shit! exactly what I stepped and slid in all the way to the water.

Frank hit the water running. "I'm too old for this shit!" I yelled.

I pulled Frank back to the bank, picked up the cooler and blanket, and we went to the car. Thank God, for leather seats!

We drove back to the hotel and prepared for our baths. We took a short nap, and later I cleaned up the car. On my way back, I ate supper and brought a scrap plate back for Frank.

A short walk, and we're settling down for the night. I told Frank I needed to stay busy and not dwell on this disease.

Nevertheless, every time I took my medicine, I was reminded that I was living on borrowed time. Frank was older now, and I prayed that he would die first. I knew that no one would love, or take care of him like I do.

I reached in the tattered bag and pulled out my little red coin purse. I always kept my change in that purse. I told Andrew that it was cuss money. The price I paid for saying ugly words. When I paid the price, it couldn't be a penny!

When Andrew took the coins he said, "Mamma, you've been cussing a lot!" He would smile, and I would promise to do better.

If Andrew wasn't home, Luke got the money. Luke would bring my purse and say, "Money mamma!" When he found the red coin purse, he would open it, pour out the coins and touch them all.

Sometimes he would put them in his pocket. Usually, I put them in a baggie. Once he had the coins, he put the coin purse back and mentioned it no more.

One day both boys' were home, and I told them to share. Andrew gave Luke the nickels and kept the rest for himself. I looked at Andrew, and he said "That's fair mamma!" It made me wonder how he got a "B" in math!

I put the red coin purse back in the tattered bag,

turned out the lights and wept.

How could I be so selfish and think only of myself? I said my prayers, kissed Frank on the nose and tried to sleep. I learned a lesson about kindness. Tomorrow would find me a different person.

Chapter 4
The Baseball Cap

This was going to be a great day. I decided to take Frank to the ocean. White sand and long walks on the beach.

Frank and I took our usual walk. We stopped by the lobby, I got coffee and two cinnamon rolls. When we got back to the room, we ate and proceeded to check out.

Our journey would take about eight hours. Hopefully, I could find us a place on the beach. Several hours later, I got off the highway, for a bathroom break and lunch.

As we drove through this small town, I was in shock! There was not one fast food place in town. A sign caught my eye. It read, "Two Choices, Take It or Leave It."

Finally, a place to eat, maybe! I parked the car and started inside to order. A sign on the door said, "Pets are Welcome." I knew better, but what the hell!

It was a small restaurant that seated about thirty people. Frank and I walked in, and he greeted everyone at every table. I placed our order and found us a place to wait. So far, so good!

Everything was going fine until a cat came around the corner. I grabbed Frank's lead just about the time it ran out. When I got him stopped, the older lady a few tables down was wearing her tea and spaghetti!

Her husband was screaming! "Damn close this time!"

The owner walked over with our order and said, "It's alright, this happens quiet often. My cat, Mighty Mouse, likes the challenge and always gets away."

I paid for our order, and as we walked out the door, I thought to myself, "Nobody will ever believe this. I'm having trouble believing it myself!"

We sat outside and ate lunch. Then I walked Frank

until he did his business. With that out of the way, we got back in the car, and were on our way.

Late that afternoon, we arrived in Gulf Shores. I rolled the windows down so that Frank could smell the ocean. I found a hotel, checked us in, and when all our stuff was in the room, I took Frank to the beach.

He was uncertain of the feel of sand. We walked to the waters edge where he got his first taste of salt water. He shook his head and backed up.

Finally, he eased into the water, but wasn't prepared for the wave that was coming. It covered him up and rolled him over. He loved it! Right back in the water he went. This moment, was worth the drive!

Thirty minutes later, we were both worn out so we went to our room, got a bath and took a nap.

When I woke up, it was time for dinner. I ate in the hotel restaurant and brought back a scrap plate for Frank. He couldn't stop looking out the window. The beach was where he wanted to be!

As we walked along the water's edge, Frank saw his first sand crab. As it began to bury itself, Frank tried to dig it out. As he dug for that one another one appeared, Frank's work would be in vain.

There were many people walking their dogs on the beach. A neat sight to see for those of us that lived in the city. As we continued our walk, we found a beach house for rent. This place would be perfect for a week, and I would call about it when we got back to the room.

The sun was beginning to set and how magnificent it was! It was almost blinding as the rays of the sun reflected off of the water.

We got back to the room, and I called about the beach house and was lucky enough to rent it for a week. Today was a good day! It felt strange to be happy, with thoughts of death coming soon.

I would hold on to this moment of happiness and pray for a few more. Funny how life reminds us of our blessings.

Frank climbed up on the bed and stretched out. I took my medicine and reached for the tattered bag. I opened it and pulled out Andrew's baseball cap.

It was blue and orange with the letter "S" and a lightning bolt running through the center of it. This symbol represented the Chargers. The baseball team that Andrew played for in high school. His number was "25."

There was one game that I will never forget. It was the bottom of the ninth inning, we were down by one run, but we had last bat!

Our first batter up struck out. The second batter flied out to center field. The third batter got a base hit and was safe at first base. The fourth batter hit a long ball to left field. Two runners on and two outs!

Andrew was on deck. His mom, and I were sitting behind the back stop at home plate. As he walked toward the batters box, he looked at us and smiled.

The first pitch was a strike. The second pitch was a ball. The third pitch he tipped foul. The count was two strikes and one ball. Talk about a lot of pressure! It was on Andrew!

I yelled, "Stayin alive with 25!"

The pitcher fired that next ball, and when Andrew swung his bat, that ball was gone!!! The ball hit the center field fence, both runners scored, and Andrew was on second base.

Andrew wasn't much of a runner, but we blamed that on his size fifteen shoes! It was a win and a great game, especially for Andrew.

I loved the game of baseball. It brought back memories of when I played softball. I was pretty good, myself!

I hope Andrew will always remember how much I love him and cherish the time we spent together.

I put his baseball cap back in the tattered bag. Said my prayers, and kissed Frank on his nose.

There was so much of his life that I would miss. I will always remember his beautiful smile, even with his braces, and his sky blue eyes that captured my heart. Thank you, Andrew, for all we have shared.

Chapter 5
The Two Chocolate Moons.

Frank and I walked on the beach early this morning, and he saw his first sea gull, but what got his attention was a sea turtle. Frank sniffed and pawed at it, until it headed for the water.

Frank swam after it until it was out of his sight, and then he swam back to shore. He was tired and ready for breakfast so we went back to our room, ate, and packed our things for the move to the beach house.

When we pulled in the drive, it was perfect! Especially the deck that faced the ocean. We would make some memories here our last days together. I was tired and the pain was more frequent.

I took everything in the house, and went to the grocery store to pick up things we needed. As soon as I got back, I put everything away and called my family.

Everyone was fine, and they wanted to know when we were coming home. I told them it would be soon and left it at that. After we hung up, I thought to myself, how long would the word, home, have meaning for me?

Should I go home and tell them the truth? Not yet.

I poured myself a glass of wine, and Frank and I went out on the deck. Watching the ocean was peaceful, and Frank enjoyed watching the people walking on the beach. He greeted them all with a bark and wagging tail.

Warm sunshine and a cool breeze were perfect ingredients for a nap. I set my glass down and closed my eyes. I awoke to Frank growling. There was a dog standing at the foot of the deck.

It was a gray and black Schnauzer with the wildest mustache you've ever seen. Frank was accepting of this dog and that surprised me.

All of a sudden, I heard someone calling, "Ollie, get back here!" As the voice got closer it seemed familiar. When I saw the man's face, I couldn't believe it! It was Bill. He and his wife, Vickie, were old friends of mine.

Years ago I bought a log cabin that was built by Bill. He introduced me to Vickie, and we became good friends. They would come and visit at the cabin and bring their dog, Ollie. Frank and Ollie became friends.

When I saw Vickie, we hugged like sisters. She retired from teaching school after thirty years. They had rented the beach house next door.

Both of their dogs, Ollie and Max, were with them. Miles and years had separated us. It would be great sharing time together again. We decided to cook out later and reminisce.

What a great evening this was going to be. The sky was alive with stars, there was a cool ocean breeze, and friends to share it with. We talked for hours, while Frank and Ollie did their usual and get in trouble.

Max was older and wiser, he just watched. When Bill and Vickie left, Frank and I went inside to get ready for bed. I wondered why they had come back in my life again. I had no answer, but I was glad.

I took my medicine, and we climbed in to bed. I reached for the tattered bag knowing that time was slipping away, and I wanted to remember while I could.

I pulled out a picture of Luke and Sippi, he was my beloved Jack Russell that died many years ago. I laughed out loud! I called this picture, "The Two Chocolate Moons!"

When Luke came to visit at the cabin, he loved to play outside, especially, in Sippi's swimming pool. We would pull his diaper off, put on his sunblock, and let him go!

Luke couldn't say Sippi, he called him Pissy. I kept Sippi's pool in an area that had very little grass. Needless to say, it got muddy quickly.

Sippi and Luke were running toward the pool. Luke fell down and Sippi followed. They were both covered in mud. Luke stepped in the pool and so did Sippi.

Luke bent over to wash the mud off of his hands, and we laughed until, we almost cried. We got a full moon shot of both their muddy butts!

We cleaned them up, ate lunch, and hoped they would lay down and take a nap. Everywhere Luke went he took his favorite toy, Tig Tig. Luke would taunt Sippi with Tig Tig, and Sippi tried his best to get it every time.

When Sippi did get it, I would have to chase him down and get it back. Sippi had two toy boxes of his own. Luke would go through both toy boxes and smell all the toys. We never could figure out why he did that.

Sippi had a Spiderman toy and Luke wanted it! His mom said, "Let Luke have that toy. Sippi won't miss it." She put it in Luke's bag to take home, turned to Sippi and said, "Thank you!"

Luke climbed up on the couch, and Sippi curled up at his feet. We enjoyed the peace and quiet. My two babies, Luke and Sippi, how funny they are together.

I put the picture back in the tattered bag and turned out the light. I have been so blessed and am so thankful. Good-night Sippi, I still love and miss you.

Chapter 6
My Children

The next morning while we were on our walk. We came upon a neat seaside cafe. The sign read, "Mel's, People are welcome, as well as their pets. We serve them all with no regrets!"

The owner, Mel, was sitting outside with her five dogs. She welcomed Frank and I as if we were old friends. She offered me a cup of coffee and gave Frank a dog biscuit. The perfect breakfast for both of us.

Mel had an outside area set up perfectly for pets. There was a constant running sprinkler to cool down the dogs, and a trough of cool water for them to drink.

Mel seemed to be a good lady with a kind heart. Not to mention a booming business. We visited for a while then said our good-byes. No doubt that we would be back.

We were on our way back to the beach house when Frank spotted Bill lying on a blanket by the water. I turned him loose, and he ran toward Bill. Ollie saw Frank coming and ran to meet him.

They both got to Bill at the same time. The next thing I heard was Bill yelling, "What the hell!" Bill was furious! Frank and Ollie had turned his drink over, and covered his freshly oiled body with sand.

Vickie and I would hear about this drama for days. To make things worse, Ollie got Bill's cigarettes and started toward the water!

The louder Bill yelled at Ollie, the faster he ran. People were watching and laughing and that really made Bill mad! He looked at Vickie and I and screamed, "Y'all need to get a grip on your dogs." We laughed until we almost cried!

Bill and his drama. We had laughed about it for years. He spent more money on his face than either one of us. The creams, injections and sweat pills to clean out his pores.

Bill always said, “When I get fifty, I will still look twenty!”

A walk on the beach sounded like a good idea. The moon was full and the stars were shining bright. The sand was warm and the water was cool. The dogs chased the waves as they rolled back in to the ocean.

When we got back to the beach house, we said our good-nights and got ready for bed. Frank got a snack, and I was feeling so bad that I took a double dose of my medicine.

I opened the tattered bag, pulled out a picture of my children and tears filled my eyes.

Both of them had blonde hair and blue eyes, but very different personalities. My daughter is tender hearted and head strong. My son is up for anything life brings and never meets a stranger.

When they were small children, money was tight and times were hard. Bills were paid first and groceries came last.

I felt that I was doing the best I could. I realized that I had failed them and myself. Bad choices and stupid decisions I realized too late. If the truth was known, my mother was the strength that held our family together.

I was a single parent in my early twenties. Taking care of my children left little time for myself. I loved them, and hoped they loved me. I expected more from them than I ever gave. Providing the simple necessities left little for extras.

Working six and seven days a week seemed to be the only way to get ahead, but it came at a great price. I missed them growing up. They always asked for more, but accepted what we had.

My mother was always there to help us, and we couldn't have made it without her help. I had grown up poor and wanted better for my family.

As time went on, and I made a better living our lives got better. In the years that followed, we went from a life of surviving to a life of comfort.

My children grew into adults and started lives of their own. I know they remembered their desires and dreams that didn't come true, but are able to do more for their children.

Love should be enough, but it's not. I can no longer hold them in my arms, but I will always carry them in my heart.

Chapter 7
The Medal

It had been a long night, and I was tired of fighting the bed, so I got up and made a pot of coffee. It was four thirty in the early morning, and the moon was shining a pale light on the ocean.

Homesickness and loneliness, was it worth it? Why was I here?

Frank was asleep at the foot of the bed. I fixed me a cup of coffee, and decided to take a walk on the beach under the moonlight.

As I walked toward the pier there was a small wooden boat pulled up on the sand. Though I didn't see anyone, I heard voices. I hesitated to proceed, but I walked on.

The voices were soft and the words were romantic. That led me to believe that a couple was making love in that boat, or so I thought!

I told myself to turn around and go back, but before I could they raised up. I was speechless! That couple had to be in their seventies! They saw me and began to laugh. They introduced themselves as Dick and Laura.

Laura said, "We made a promise to each other to come back at least once a year, to the place we first made love, fifty years ago. I thought to myself, "who's on top," is really important in this situation!

I couldn't wait to share that with Bill and Vickie!

I had been single for many years, my life was sometimes lonely, but another failed relationship wasn't an option. I missed companionship, but was unwilling to make any type of commitment.

That episode with Dick and Laura made me think of the crazy places I had sex. For me, it was in the front seat of a sports car, since there was no back seat, with a very tall man!

A co-worker of mine, an older man we called, Pop once told me that the best sex he ever had was during the spin cycle on top of the washing machine! That gave new meaning to the spin cycle!

I laughed all the way back to the beach house. I remembered that old song, “By the light of the silvery moon.” This morning I saw two, old moons! It was going to be a great day!

I walked up on the deck, and Frank was sitting at the door. The minute I opened it he ran straight for the ocean. The sun was coming up and what a sunrise it was!

Vickie and I were going shopping today, and Bill was dog sitting. We decided to walk to town, it was only a few blocks. The sidewalks and shops were crowded with people. My mind wasn’t on shopping, but I put on a happy face and tried to enjoy our trip.

It was lunchtime when we got back. Bill and the dogs were on the deck. They left and we went inside. I was tired and wanted to take a nap.

I laid across the bed and thought, how unpredictable life truly is and there are no answers. I didn’t want to sleep because those were minutes I couldn’t go back and get.

I was haunted by my decision to lie to my family. I cried more about this decision than any other in my life. I got up, got over my pity party and decided to take Frank out on the deck.

There was a man walking his Dachshund down the beach. Before I knew it, Frank jumped over the railing and ran to join them.

“No, Frank, No!” I yelled, but it was too late!

He jumped up on this man to greet him and knocked

him down. It scared his dog, and she began to bark. I helped him up and apologized for Frank's behavior. He just laughed, and they went on their way.

It was almost supper time when we got back. I asked God to let me be a part of whatever and whenever as long as I could. I still had a good life, I was alive.

Bill was putting steaks on the grill, Vickie was making a salad, and all I had to do was get the wine. We ate out on the deck and divided the scraps for the dogs. We made it an early evening, everyone was tired.

When they left, I loaded the dishwasher and went to the tub for a long soak. I took my medicine and suffered in silence. I have tried to look on the bright side instead of complaining about my circumstances.

My situation was hopeless. It's not fair or right, but sometimes life turns out differently than we planned or expected.

We don't pay attention to things in our life until they aren't right. I strive for understanding, but it's beyond my grasp. At times I wonder why I keep trying. Carrying this burden finds me exhausted and discouraged. I know it's because I'm not living the truth in my life.

I reached in the tattered bag and pulled out my medal. It read, "Instrumental Award and Outstanding Service." I was awarded that medal for playing the flute in the high school band.

When I started junior high school, I had a plan. If I joined the band and played sports, I could go to events on the school bus. My mom didn't have a car, so I was limited to when and where I could go.

I remember the day I got my flute, band uniform and my white gloves. I couldn't wait to show my mom! I took my flute home every day and practiced until mom got home from work.

If I practiced after supper, I would take a lamp into my closet to read my music sheet, and close the door to give my mom a break! She never complained about my off key playing. She encouraged me and showed great patience.

I loved playing at pep rallies and ball games. Sometimes we performed at half-time. My best memory was at the Strawberry Festival and Parade.

That event was at the end of the school year, and we were gone all day. We marched in the parade and then went to the carnival. There were rides, games and cotton candy!

That year our school band won first place, and I won a big white teddy bear at the carnival. It was a great day and the perfect way to end the school year. I was a part of something to be remembered, and very proud of it.

My mother taught me early on, life is not just about the victories, there will be sacrifice and many unanswered questions. Contentment has little to do with what we have or lack.

She always said, “It’s easier to walk through an open door instead of forcing my way through a closed one.”

How did you get so smart, mom? I hope you passed some of it on to me. I put my medal back in the bag, kissed Frank on the nose and turned out the light.

Chapter 8
A Man of God.

The next morning, we went next door to tell Bill and Vickie good-bye. The dogs played on the beach and took their last swim in the ocean. We loaded our cars and prepared for the drive home.

We promised to stay in touch more often. We followed each other down the interstate for about one hundred miles then, Bill and Vickie got off.

I drove a while longer, found a roadside park and pulled off, for a break and some lunch. I fixed myself a coke then got a bowl of water and some food for Frank. He didn't seem hungry, maybe he was tired.

We got back on the road and drove until late afternoon. I finally found a small town with a hotel, so we got off the highway, found the hotel and checked in. The name of this place was "Just Like Home" and there was a restaurant next door called, "The Kitchen Table."

I unloaded the car, and we took a walk around the town. There was an old train depot beside the train track. We climbed up the steps, and I sat down on the bench.

The town square was across the tracks. I could see chairs and benches in front of the stores. Probably a gathering place for customers and friends. There was a hardware store, grocery store, jail and a barber shop.

A man was sitting in front of the barber shop playing a harmonica. He looked like he could use a hot bath and a good meal. His gray beard needed a trim and his clothes were dirty and about two sizes too big.

He wore a straw hat to shield his face from the sun and had on a pair of worn out boots. Could he be a hobo waiting on the train to his next destination?

Frank and I crossed the tracks to listen to him play. As we approached the man, he stopped playing and said, “Hello, come and sit for a while.”

He rubbed Frank’s head and tears filled his eyes. He told about his dog, Boxcar, how he got sick and died, and this man had been alone ever since.

“Most folks don’t stop and talk.” he said. “My name is Jumpin Joe.”

He began to tell his sad story. He left home as a young man and even though he missed his family, he never went back.

“Too, many bad memories, I just try to get through the day,” he whispered with his head down.

I told him that we had to go and wished him good luck. I put a twenty dollar bill in his hand, and he thanked me. He asked if there was a song that he could play for me.

I replied, “Play me your favorite song.”

As we walked away he began to play *Amazing Grace.* I sang along as the tears ran down my face. I loved that song, especially the third verse.

“Through many dangers, toils and snares, I have already come.

Tis grace that brought me safe thus far, and grace will lead me home.

A train was his Cadillac, and a boxcar was his home. A broken man, so all alone, who simply wanted kindness and a friend.

I took Frank back to the room, and went next door to order our supper. When I walked in the restaurant, I asked for a menu. I have never seen anything like it, or ever will again!

Gather Round The Kitchen Table

Soups On!

Owner-Mr. Wayne

Cookin-Bakin-Ms. Jodie

Breakfast- Bacon-Ham-Sausage

Hogs raised and prepared by Mr. Wayne, slopped twice a day.

Eggs: Any way you want them. Gathered daily from Mr. Wayne's chicken houses.

Flap Jacks- 5 to a stack, homemade Maple syrup or Sorghum

Grits- ground from Mr. Wayne's corn, cooked to perfection. Not runny or thick.

Homemade Buttermilk Biscuits- Hand rolled daily. Ms. Jodie makes ten pans every morning. When their gone, we serve toast.

Homemade Butter- Milk from Mr. Wayne's cows. Churned and salted to taste.

Jellies and Jams- Fruit from Mr. Wayne's orchard. Cooked and canned by Ms. Jodie.

Jelly

Jams

Pear Preserves

Apple

Blackberry

Peach

Strawberry

Muscadine

Plum

Drinks

Coffee- Hot and strong, no decaf, just the real stuff

Milk- Fresh daily from Mr. Wayne's cows

Orange Juice-Frozen, Ms. Jodie ain't got time to squeeze all those oranges and cook, too!

Breakfast plate and drink- $3.99

Drinks

Iced Tea- sweet or unsweet, lemon upon request

Ice water- Mr. Wayne's well water, no bottled water

Sodas- Coke, Pepsi, Dr. Pepper, Orange or Grape. All in the drink box-50 cents a bottle. (Believe I'd drink water at that price)

Cornbread- baked fresh daily in cast iron skillet

Yeast Rolls- homemade, fresh daily, hand rolled, and kept in frig for 12 hours to let yeast rise. (Ms. Jodie's secret recipe and she ain't tellin!)

Lunch and Dinner plate- $5.00

Fried Chicken- Raised and prepared by Mr. Wayne. He don't use no chemicals and feeds em twice a day. Best eatin birds in town!

Hamburger Steak and Gravy-Cows raised and prepared by Mr. Wayne. Grain fed, grazed in good pasture grass. Gravy is Ms. Jodie's secret recipe.

Tater or Sweet Taters-Grown and dug by Mr. Wayne. No brown spots. Creamed, fried or baked.

Corn on the Cob-Planted and picked by Mr. Wayne. Yellow or white. The secret is in the scarecrow!

Turnip Greens or Purple Hull Peas-Planted and picked by Mr. Wayne. Seasoned with fatback.

Friday Nite Catfish 5pm-7pm $6.00

Mississippi pond raised in Mr. Wayne's 5 acre pond. Always fresh, never frozen, grain fed.

Whole catfish, or fillet

Fixins- All ingredients from Mr. Wayne's garden

Tomato Relish-canned and stored in the root cellar. Sets three months before serving.

Hushpuppies-made from scratch. Secrets in the grease

Slaw-fresh and crunchy, a little bit spicy!

Vidalia Onions-easy on the breath.

Desserts $1.00

All deserts homemade by Ms. Jodie using her secert recipes. Mouth watering, knee slapping GOOD!

Puddings- Banana, Bread, and Rice

Pies- Apple, Pecan, Chocolate and Lemon

Cakes- Caramel and Chocolate

Homemade Ice Cream- we fudge a little bit here, can't get anyone to sit on the churn!

We enjoyed your company. Hope you enjoyed your meal.

Y'all come back now!

I took my order to the room and shared with Frank, even the Apple Pie. That was the best meal I had eaten in a long time. We needed a walk because both our tummies were full.

When we got back, I took a bath and Frank climbed up on the bed and stretched out. I rubbed him down his back and told him that I loved him and we would soon be home.

I prepared to take my medicine and realized that I was almost out. I debated whether to refill it. It wasn't working very well and it usually made me sick. I knew I was getting worse.

I was losing weight and it really showed in my face. When I looked in the mirror, I didn't see the face I saw a month ago. This disease was taking my life.

How much longer would I live? I wasn't ready to die, but that was out of my control. Who would love Frank? I can't imagine someone giving him a life similar to what he has now. It breaks my heart to think about it.

I reached in the tattered bag and pulled out a card. It was brother, Jimmy Latimer's business card from Redeemer Evangelical Church. He was my preacher for many years.

He had helped and guided me in difficult situations. I love the fact that he tells it like it is.

Brother Jimmy was preaching on the book of, Job, and his sermon changed my life. How long I had waited for an answer to something that had haunted me. Not knowing what it would be, or when it would come, but that day my question was answered!

I never knew my real father, but always wanted to. It broke my heart to think my father didn't want to know me or be a part of my life.

How could he have treated me as if I didn't exist? I'd been left with years of wondering. Evidently, my life meant nothing to him, and responsibility was something he wasn't going to accept.

I don't blame myself, but he got a free ride on my broken heart. He was invisible. Daddy's little girl and Father's Day had no meaning for me.

I tried to find him many times, but always failed. I could never thank my mom enough, for doing and being it all for me.

One Sunday morning as Brother Jimmy was preaching, I finally got it! I had always known my father, my Heavenly Father, God. He was always there for me, loving and watching over me.

Though I called on Him, many times in my life, I never figured it out until then. There is no greater father than God!

Brother Jimmy is a dear friend and one of God's finest men. I didn't tell him about my illness, maybe when I get home. I put his card back in the bag and prayed for both of us.

I was scared and ready to go home. Maybe sleep would come. I turned out the light and prayed that this night, my Father was with me.

My life was ending, and for the first time I enjoyed using the word, Father.

Chapter 9
The Old Home Place

I took Frank for his morning walk, and when we got back, I fed and watered him. I loaded the car, put Frank in the front seat and checked out.

I stopped and got gas; we were three hundred miles from home. I was ready to get back, but not ready to have the discussion with my family that was coming.

Frank curled up in the front seat and went to sleep. It was unlike him to be so still. I know he's older and tired; and I hope that's all it is. I was beginning to worry. Truth is, I've been worried for days.

My precious Frank, I can't imagine life without him. He had become my best friend, and I loved him so.

I needed to hear some music so I put in a CD by Charles Heinz, the music director at Redeemer Evangelical Church. I cried and sang along with the music.

My life was coming to an end, and I wasn't prepared. I still didn't know how to tell my family. Who will take care of Frank?

We were about fifty miles from my home town, Duck Hill, Mississippi when I decided to exit off and visit my old home place once more. What would I find, or feel when I got there.

When we got to town, I pulled over and parked beside the railroad track. I got Frank out, and we walked around. The statue of the Chief Duck was still standing there. It represented the Duck Indians, who lived in this town and on the hill years ago.

The town hadn't changed much at all, and my memory is from when I was a small child. There was a country store, hardware store and the jail which was a small trailer.

We started back to the car, and when we got to the statue, Frank hiked his leg and pee-peed on it! I thought I would die, or go to jail! We got back in the car and started down the old two lane highway.

I turned off at the Red Hill sign knowing this road would take us to the family cemetery. All the roads from now on would be gravel. I rolled down the window so Frank could experience the smells of the country.

When we got to the church and cemetery, it was as I remembered it. I got Frank out, and we walked around. The rows of wooden tables and benches were still under the big shade trees.

Every Mother's Day, relatives would come, bringing food for lunch and flowers for their families' graves. We called this Memorial Day and dinner on the ground.

The tables would be covered with home cooking and lots of it! We would spend the day sharing old memories and making new ones.

I fixed Frank a bowl of water, and hooked him up under the shade tree, opened the gate to the cemetery and began my walk. Members of my family from the eighteen hundreds until now are buried there.

The grass was cut and every grave had flowers. It looked so nice and peaceful. Every time I came here sadness filled my heart, and I always cried when I visited my grandfather's grave.

He was the only man in my life as a child, and I loved him so. I knelt down, touched his headstone and said, "I love you and I will see you soon."

I walked out of the cemetery and closed the gate. I loaded Frank up, and down the gravel road we went. We were headed toward the old home place, I was going home. I lived many places, but this was my home.

One more curve in the road and there it was. It looked pretty good to be one hundred years old. The grass had been cut, and my grandmother's rose bushes were blooming.

I could hardly wait to let Frank out and sit on the front porch. No leash this time he could run free! I opened the car door, and off he went.

I got his water bowl out, filled it with fresh water, and set it on the porch. I set down on the top step and watched him explore.

He was having a blast! He finally wore himself down and came to the porch for a drink. He laid down beside me and took a nap. Memories of my childhood days there flooded my mind.

I loved the time I spent at my grandparents' farm. I spent most of my time with my grandfather. He was the greatest, and I loved him so very much.

When we didn't have the money to ride the train home, my grandfather would come to Memphis, and pick us up in his old Ford. It didn't have a heater, so my grandmother would send blankets for us to cover up with when it was cold. I always sat in the front seat next to my grandfather.

As soon as we got to the house, we unloaded our things, and our adventures began. At Christmas time, my grandfather would go to the woods and cut a Christmas tree. After he got it to the house, we would decorate it and sometimes shoot fireworks off the front porch.

Spring and summer brought new adventures. Most afternoons my grandfather would make a freezer of ice cream. My grandmother mixed up the ingredients, poured the mixture into the cylinder and placed it in the churn packed with salt and ice.

My grandfather turned the handle on the side until the ice cream got hard. Someone had to sit on top of the freezer to keep it steady. That was my job! Thank goodness for the two towels between me and the ice!

I remembered two accidents that I had while I was at the farm. One day I got an itch on the bottom of my foot. There was a walkway made of wooden planks leading up to the front porch. I thought that would be a great place to scratch my itch. Bad choice!

I rubbed my foot so hard against the plank that I got a splinter in it, and no one could get it out. My grandfather took me to the hospital, and the doctor told him, I would have to be put to sleep for him to get the splinter out. It was real deep!

In those days a doctor poured ether on a pad and placed it over your nose to put you to sleep. When I woke up, I was sick to my stomach, and my foot really hurt! I knew that I would never do that again!

My next episode was the worst! My grandparents owned land on both sides of the road. My grandfather built a bridge and dug out underneath it, so the cows could graze on either side of the road.

I was jumping up and down on the bridge, while throwing rocks at the cows when a board gave way. Before I knew it, one leg was stuck between two boards, and I couldn't get out.

I was too far from the house to call for help. Worst of all, there were cows under the bridge, and I was afraid of cows! I was afraid one might bite me. I didn't like cows!

My grandfather came down the road and found me. He got my leg out and said, "We'll fix the bridge tomorrow." We laughed all the way back to the house.

Sometimes, he would fill the wagon with salt blocks,

hook it to the tractor, and take the salt blocks to the pasture for the cows to lick. One day we found a dead cow in the pasture.

My grandfather put chains around it and drug it back up in the woods, for the buzzards to eat. Buzzards are big, ugly birds, but they do serve a purpose.

I always wanted to shoot my grandfather's rifle. I bugged him about it all the time. I finally got my wish one day. Little did I know that the rifle was a 30.06!

He put a can on the fence post and loaded the gun. He handed it to me and said, "Be careful and good luck." I lined the gun site up with the can, put the rifle butt against my shoulder and pulled the trigger! When I opened my eyes, I saw the sky!

My ears were ringing, and my shoulder was killing me. Worst of all, the can was still on the fence post. My grandfather asked if I wanted to try one more time. Needless to say, I never shot that rifle again!

There were chores to do every day on the farm. First thing in the morning, I went to the chicken coops and gathered the eggs. My grandfather kept a King snake out there to keep the rats from stealing the eggs. That snake scared me to death!

One morning the snake was between me and the coops. I took a hoe and tried to kill it. My grandfather yelled, "Gal, don't you kill my snake!" I almost got a spanking, but I hated that snake and planned to kill it one day.

After breakfast I went to the barn and worked on the corn. There were three cribs at one end of the barn. I shucked the corn and put the shucks in a straw basket. These would be fed to the cows in the late afternoon.

Next, I would grind the corn off the cob using the old

grinder and put it in a bucket for chicken feed. I threw the corn cobs in a special crib. They served a needed purpose, they were around long before toilet paper!

Before lunch, I went to the garden and gathered the ripe vegetables. On my way back to the house, I stopped at the orchard and picked some apples. If I wasn't in the field at lunchtime, I got to ring the dinner bell!

That let everyone in the field know that lunch was ready and on the table. After lunch, I went to my favorite place to take a nap. The old swing that hung in the open hallway of the house. I laid down in the swing, and pushed myself with my feet. I swung myself to sleep every time.

Every afternoon, the old man in his wagon came looking for handouts. My grandmother would give him anything she was throwing away. He let me climb up in his wagon and look through his finds.

In the early evening, I took my basket of corn shucks to the cow lane and dumped them for the cows, always before they got there because I was afraid of cows!

Then I got a bucket of corn and fed the chickens. I threw out the corn, a handful at a time until the bucket was empty. Sometimes, one of the chickens would try to peck me. I got my revenge on Sunday when I got to pick the chicken that was Sunday dinner!

A number three washtub was filled with water every morning and placed on the back porch in the sun.

The sun warmed the water during the day, and that was my bathtub in the evening. I dried off quickly, put on my pajamas, and got ready to listen to the radio until bedtime.

At bedtime, a slop jar (pee-pot) was put in the bedroom in case I needed to use the bathroom during the night. The outhouse was a long walk down the hill. No electricity and a wild imagination of what I might see made me thankful for the pot!

When I got up that next morning, I took the pot to the outhouse and dumped it. My grandmother saved newspapers and catalogues to use as toilet paper. Before I took them down the hill, I tore out certain pages and cut the people out for paper dolls.

When it was time for me to go home, my grandfather would take me to town the day before and let me shop. There wasn't much money, usually about two dollars, but I always found something to buy.

****

In 1962, I was devastated by the death of my grandfather. My uncle had driven him to the doctor, and on their way home he fell over against the car door and died. The only man in my life was gone.

In those days when someone died, the body was prepared and brought back to the house until the burial.

A casket stand was brought in for the body to be placed on, and black draperies were hung at the windows in the room where the body was viewed.

Family and friends came to pay their respects, and also brought food and desserts to help feed the family. The day of the funeral the hearse came to the house, and took his body to the church.

That was the first funeral I attended. Why did it have to be my grandfather? My time on the farm would forever be changed. Since he was gone, I didn't want to go back.

Years later when my grandmother died, her assets were divided, and my mother acquired his trunk, and the old bedroom suit from the north room. Years later, she gave those things to me.

When I opened his trunk, the first thing I saw was his

hat. I took it out and held it close to my heart and cried. He always wore that hat. The history of my family was in that trunk, and I would cherish those things forever.

****

My memories made me feel good, and I decided to go exploring. I walked up to the door, and it wasn't locked so I went inside. Frank was right behind me, and we began to look around.

Almost empty, no pictures or voices made it seem strange, but it was still home. I decided to spend the night, probably for the last time.

It was late and too dark to drive. I went to the car, got our things, some food, a couple of blankets and the tattered bag. We ate and went to the porch to watch the sunset.

I began to feel sick. I threw up and noticed some blood. I took my medicine without hesitation. I was scared! Would we make it back home?

We went inside, and Frank jumped up on the old couch and stretched out. I covered him up and pushed two chairs together for myself. I reached in the tattered bag and pulled out a picture of my mother. That was the perfect memory because that was her home place, too.

****

I remembered the day she called me and said she wasn't feeling well, but she was going to the doctor for a check-up on Tuesday. She called me Tuesday evening and said, "There was a problem with her treadmill test results, and they wanted to schedule a heart catheter test on Thursday."

I told her that I would come and stay as long as she needed me. I left my home at four a.m. Thursday morning, drove seventy miles to her house, picked her up and drove to the hospital.

I prepared to spend the day and take her home later that afternoon. She went to surgery, and I went to the waiting room.

A few hours later the surgery nurse called and said the test was over, and mom was going to a room. I went to the room and waited with mom for the results. Five hours later, the first round of bad news came.

A nurse took me out into the hall and said, "Your mother isn't going home today. The doctor would be in soon with her results."

My mom kept asking where the doctor was. She wanted to go home. What would those tests reveal? Would we be prepared?

My mom had always been there for me, now it was my turn to be there for her. How long before we left that place? Surely, it wouldn't be too long, I would get caught up on things when I got home.

The doctor walked in the room, sat down in the chair, and gave us the results. My mom had eighty percent blockage in three arteries of her heart, and one of her carotid arteries in her neck was ninety percent blocked.

If both surgeries weren't done at the same time, she could have a stroke. The doctor felt that she could survive both surgeries, but there were no guarantees because she was seventy seven years old.

In addition, both of her legs would be cut from knee to ankle to remove good veins to use in her heart. Her options were limited; it would be a dangerous and lengthy operation.

The blockage was too massive for her to go home before surgery. She had to stay in the hospital through the week-end and the surgery would be done Monday morning. We listened while he explained the procedures.

He asked mom what she wanted to do? She replied, "Do them both at the same time." What happened next shocked us both!

The doctor said, "Let's pray." We held hands, and the doctor asked God to guide his hands during surgery and watch over my mom.

When he left the room, my mom cried. I knew she was scared, but she said, "If God was ready to take her home, she was ready to go."

I wanted to scream! Surely, God wouldn't let her die. She was my lifeline, and I needed her. I love her-this can't be happening!

Mom and I talked about many things that afternoon and through the evening. I decided to stay the night. Needless to say, that old couch left alot to be desired, but it was better than sleeping in a chair.

We didn't get much sleep, nurses were in and out most of the night. The next morning, the regimen of tests and blood work began. I decided to leave that afternoon, get my things in order at home and come back on Sunday. Friends and church members would keep her company until I got back.

When I got back Sunday afternoon, I parked my car, prayed and cried before I went inside. This crisis was something neither money nor my knowledge could fix. God needed to fix the problem, and let me get back home to my life. At that point I felt in control.

I walked into her room as confidently, and as upbeat as I could. Brother Kevin, Mom's pastor, and church members had visited and prayed over the week-end.

When mom and I were alone, we were faced with questions and decisions. I tried to console and assure mom that the surgery would be successful.

Mom's faith in God was without question. Later that evening the doctor came in and prepared us for the procedure and recovery time, if all went well. Before he left, we held hands again and prayed. That was the longest night of my life. I can't imagine how she really felt.

Early that next morning, they prepared mom for surgery. When they came to take her to surgery, I told her that I loved her, and I would be there when she woke up.

As they took her out of the room, I cried and prayed. Would she survive the surgery? What would I do if she didn't? I gathered our things and went to the Intensive Care Waiting Room.

I decided to take my things to the car. As I walked, tears ran down my face. How could God let this happen to a woman that loved him so much? Anger and fear were controlling my emotions.

I didn't know what to do, and I didn't want to be there. I gained my composure and went to the waiting room. I remembered the doctor's words. If all goes well, mom would be in a room in twenty four hours and could go home in four or five days.

The Intensive Care waiting room was full of recliners. I would occupy one as long as she was there. There was a small room to the side that had a coffee maker and snacks. A television mounted to the wall and a desk with two telephones. One was for incoming calls and the other phone was a direct line to surgery.

The family was updated every thirty minutes during surgery and when the patient went to recovery. The first call came for me, surgery had started and could take seven hours.

Brother Kevin and other church members were there. We all prayed for mom. I was scared, but thankful God and his people were there. It was a depressing place. Death made itself visible many times for families in that room.

The telephones rang constantly in that room. Another call came for me, Mom was stable and doing well. She had been in surgery for a few hours, but it seemed like an eternity.

I was hungry and needed to smoke, but I didn't leave the room. People were coming and going all the time. This place was full of sadness and death. Why did God bring me here?

Another call came from surgery. There were two teams of doctors' working on my mother. There were problems finding enough good veins in her legs, to replace the bad ones in her heart. She was stable.

I said a silent prayer, "God, help them save her. She's my mom, and I love her." How many other people in that room were praying the same prayer for someone they loved? Who would live or die today?

The people from Mom's church were so kind. Constantly asking if they could do anything for me. Calls from friends and family were constant.

Where was the rest of my family? I shouldn't be the only one here. I was scared and angry. Surely, God didn't bring me here to watch my mother die!

The last call came from surgery, the operation was over. Mom was stable and on her way to recovery.

My heart was racing, my eyes filled with tears, my whispered words, "Thank you, God."

Now I could make plans to get mom home, and get back to my life. We would be out of here in a few days. I left the waiting room to smoke and get some fresh air. It would be a few hours until I could see my mother.

When the four o'clock visitation came, Ms. Christine,

a lady from mom's church, went with me. As we walked the long hallway toward the double doors, I began to cry. I didn't know what to expect when I saw my mother.

The double doors opened, and we began to look for mom's room. All the rooms had glass fronts. We found her room, and I prayed for the courage to be strong. Would she be awake or strong enough to fight for her life. I needed for her to know I was there, and she wasn't alone.

There were so many machines hooked to her that I could only touch her on her forehead. I kissed her and said, "I'm here mom, surgery is over, and you're doing fine."

There was a breathing tube down her throat, so she couldn't speak. She opened her eyes, and they were black. I was devastated. She looked so bad that I felt she could die. The next twenty four hours would be critical.

Our fifteen minutes were up, and I could visit again at six o'clock. Until that moment, I had never envisioned my life without her. I thanked God, for getting her through surgery and prayed for her recovery.

Ms. Christine and I went back to the waiting room to share the news. Later that evening, mom's friends left and said they would be back tomorrow. We prayed and they left.

I left the waiting room to smoke and get dinner. When I got back to the waiting room, I got in my recliner and tried to gather my thoughts.

I sat next to a very nice lady, Mrs. Ferguson, and her son James. Her husband was a patient in Intensive Care. He was in critical condition. We began to share our reasons for being there.

It was time for the last visit of the night. I walked down the hall and waited for the doors to open. I started toward mom's room, and it almost made me sick. You could smell death.

This place was more than enough to break your heart. It took a special type of person to work here and be confronted with death daily.

When I walked into mom's room, she was awake and stable. She looked up at me, but couldn't speak because of the breathing tube down her throat. I touched her forehead, and told her that I loved her.

Mark was my mother's personal nurse, and if there was a problem he would let me know. My fifteen minutes were up, and my next visit would be in twelve hours.

Now, the waiting began. I went back to the waiting room, got in my chair, and prayed that God would get her through the night.

The waiting room was full and that damn telephone was still ringing. When the last visitors left for the night, I turned off the television and as many lights as I could.

My recliner was beside the consultation room. I didn't like being in that spot because family members and doctors were constantly making life and death decisions in that room, and I could hear them.

I took off my shoes, covered up with a blanket and prayed.

I awoke to someone touching my foot and calling my name. It was Mark. My heart was racing and my fears were running wild. He told me that my mom was in crisis, so he had called the surgeon back to the hospital.

What he did next shocked me! He said, "If you believe in prayer, you need to pray!" He took me to my mother's room, and the surgeon was sitting at the foot of the bed.

There was a problem with the carotid artery in her neck. Everything was touch and go now, he had done all that he could.

I stood beside my mother's bed thinking she might not leave this place, alive. Where was my faith? Only God knew when death would take my mother.

She looked at me as if she knew death was close. I told her everything was fine. She was at deaths door, and I was powerless to save her. Her eyes were black, and her skin was cold.

She looked at me as if to say, "Take me home." How could God let this happen? Why now?

They began to make adjustments to the machines that were keeping her alive. I was told to go back to the waiting room, and they would let me know if anything changed.

When I got back to the waiting room, the Fergusons were waiting to get a report. How kind and concerned they were. After we talked, I got back in my chair, covered up and wept silently.

Memories, of my mother's life filled my mind. I began to remember things about her journey from childhood until now. A hard and difficult life.

****

Robert and Mollie Frazier, my great grandparents, started their life as one in Duck Hill, Mississippi. With the help of family, friends and share croppers they built a home. Later, they built two more houses for the share croppers and their families.

They prepared to work the land for all it would bear. They raised cattle and hogs for meat. They prayed to survive and prosper.

My great grandparents had four children, my grandfather, Guy, was the youngest. His father died when he was nine years old. Years later, his siblings married and moved out on their own. When my great grandmother died, my grandfather decided to stay there and make that place his home.

In the state of Mississippi, when both parents are dead, all living children, inherit equal shares of the estate. My grandfather bought his siblings part of their home place. He met and married Jodie, my grandmother.

They had seven children, four boys and three girls. My mother was the first born, one of her brother's died as an infant.

Mom learned the difference between work and play early in her life. Struggling and poor, life would bring hardships not yet known. A young girl's dreams quickly turned to responsibility and sacrifice.

Land owners and share croppers had to work together in those days. One person couldn't work the fields and run the farm, too. During World War 2, most share croppers moved to the city to work in the factories. The Fox family stayed and helped work on the farm.

This family had been on this land since my great grandfather bought it. Perry was the father's name, his son's name was Clyde, Rosett and Bella were his two daughters. Perry and Rosett were deaf and mute.

Rosett taught my mother sign language so they could communicate. There were two women in the family, but mom never could remember their names. These women helped my grandmother cook and clean.

Bella and mom helped by making their famous mud pies. As mom got older, play time changed to responsibilities.

Mom cut, hauled, and stacked wood for cooking and heating in the winter time. She learned to hook up the mules and plow every other row in the cotton field alongside Perry.

Animals had to be fed, crops and vegetables had to be gathered daily. At the age of eight years old, most children went to the field to pick cotton. It was easier for them to bend over and pull the cotton bowl.

Tar was pasted on the bottom of the cotton sack to prevent it from tearing, when dragged between the rows.

Below the cotton field was a creek, better known as the swimming hole, when the cows weren't in it. It was deep enough that you could dive off the side and not hit the bottom.

At night time mom did her homework by the light from a kerosene lamp, they had no electricity. Years later, battery powered lights and radios became available. It was a special treat, at the end of the day, to sit in front of the radio and imagine life outside the farm.

At Christmas time, presents were put in chairs beside the fireplace. Mom said there was never a Christmas tree until there were grandchildren.

As a teenager, mom walked through the woods to Gwendolyn's house, her cousin, not only to visit, but to go to church. My mom joined and was baptized at the Red Hill Church of Christ. As a result my grandparents joined this church, too.

School was very important to my grandparents. All the kids walked down the gravel road to meet the bus. If the weather was bad, my grandfather would hitch up the mules to the wagon and take the kids to the bus stop.

After World War II, my grandfather talked the bus driver into coming up to the house to pick up the kids. That made their walk shorter and safer.

My mom was a very good basketball player in high school, but her greatest accomplishment was graduating Valedictorian. After graduation, mom moved to Memphis and enrolled in business school.

She lived with a Jewish family, and helped take care

of their children as part of her rent. She finished business school and moved out on her own. That was an exciting time in her life.

She always rode the bus because she didn't know how to drive and couldn't afford a car. Dreams and goals would soon pass away.

Seven years later, she became a divorced mother of two with no child support or assistance. All of her time was spent working and taking care of us.

When mom got paid, we always got to eat at the Krystal. We each got two hamburgers and a drink. I loved to sit at the counter and spin around on that stool!

After we ate, we went next door to Hogue and Knott and bought groceries. The walk home was about three blocks. We stopped several times because the sacks were heavy. The worst times were during cold weather or rain. We had no choice, since we didn't have a car and couldn't afford a cab.

We didn't shop for clothes very often, but I didn't really care. We bought most of our clothes at Kent's Dollar Store. I tried not to complain because that was the best my mom could do.

We never owned a home. We always rented. Once a week, we walked several blocks to the laundromat to wash and dry clothes. When I was about thirteen years old, mom bought a washing machine, but she couldn't afford a dryer.

In the summer time she hung clothes outside on the clothes line. In the winter, she hung them on hangers above all the doorways and in the bathroom.

The next summer, we got our first window unit air conditioner and it was great! Prior to that we only had a window fan.

I shared a bedroom with my mom, and we slept in

twin beds. Years later, my sister got married, and I got my own room! My mom bought me a canopy bed and it was like living a dream.

Saturday nights were very special. Mom always fixed my favorite meal, Chef-Boy-Ar-Dee box pizza. I have always loved it and still fix it today!

We were raised Pentecostal, we went to church on Sunday morning, Sunday evening, and Wednesday night. Missing church was not an option even though we always walked. Heat, rain, or cold.

I only remember my mom dating one man. She spent most of her life alone until we were grown. She feared that someone might be mean to us.

How many times did she cry and pray for help? I never knew the hardships she faced until years later. How blessed I was and still am to have such a wonderful mother.

****

A telephone ringing woke me up. It was five thirty a.m., and people were coming into the waiting room. I realized that Mom had made it through the night, and I could see her in thirty minutes.

Thank you, God! What would today bring? Maybe the crisis had passed. I went to the bathroom, washed my face and brushed my teeth. I was anxious to see mom.

I walked the hallway and waited for the double doors to open. I was alone, but she was still alive, and that was the most important thing right now.

I walked into the room, and she was asleep. So pale and still, after such a terrible night, but she was still holding on. I touched her forehead, and she opened her eyes. I told her that I loved her and she was doing better.

Mark, her nurse, said, “If she continues to get better, I’ll remove the breathing tube before your next visit.” That was a great sign!

It would be wonderful if she could breathe on her own. I might get home in a few days. My time was up and I was very hungry. I told mom that I would be back in two hours. I left the room, thanking God, for doing his job.

I walked outside to smoke, and on the way to my car, I broke into tears and my heart began to pound. I prayed for strength to get through another day, hoping some of our family would come.

Mom was always there for them. It made me angry that all they did was call. She had two sisters, and she needed them. She was fighting for her life with every breath.

I decided to stop answering their calls. If they wanted to know how she was, they needed to come.

Brother Kevin and some of the church members were there for the eight o'clock visit. Brother Kevin and I went to see mom. She was awake, but couldn't speak because the breathing tube was still in her throat.

He spoke a few words to mom, and then he began to pray. I bowed my head as tears ran down my face. I hoped God, was listening and answering that prayer.

Mark told us that her breathing tube would be removed if she continued to improve, and if things continued to improve she would be moved to a room in a few days.

We went back to the waiting room to give everyone an update. Ms. Ruth, a friend from the church, brought me some homemade fried Apple pies. I thanked her and said, "Those are my favorite, and I probably wouldn't share."

I went outside and smoked. I knew mom wasn't out of the woods yet, but I was hopeful. I tried to gather my thoughts and deal with my anger of being there alone.

It was almost ten o'clock, time for the next visit so I

went back to the waiting room. How humble I felt knowing God's people were supporting and comforting me.

When I walked into the room, she was propped up in the bed and the breathing tube was gone. She was awake and trying to talk. I was overjoyed!

She was saying crazy things because of the drugs. I told her the worst was over, and we would soon be home.

She looked into my eyes and said, "I'll never leave this place, I'm going to die here."

My time was up, and my next visit would be at two o'clock. I told mom I loved her and went back to share the good news. We all prayed and thanked God, for his mercy.

Neither one of mom's sisters had shown up. How could they do that? For the moment, I put my anger aside and celebrated her victory over death.

I walked outside, looked up at the sky, took a deep breath and whispered, "Thank you, God, for this miracle."

I managed to get some lunch before going back to the waiting room. If mom had a good day, maybe she would be moved tomorrow. I felt on top of the world!

Intensive Care was a very depressing place. Tragedy was all around and there was no escaping it for someone in that room. If I got mom out of here and back home. I could get back to my life.

A man from mom's church was going with me to the next visit. We walked to the double doors and waited for them to open. We had been there fifteen minutes and the doors were still closed. What was wrong?

A nurse came out and said, "There would be no visitation because a patient was in crisis." I put my hands over my face and cried. I knew in my heart, she was in trouble.

The man reminded me that she had been improving

and it could be someone else. Fear gripped my heart. Who was in crisis?

No one came to the waiting room to notify family members. Was it my mother? Four o'clock was the next visitation time if the crisis was over.

At ten minutes till four o'clock, a nurse came to the waiting room and sat down beside me. I knew, I knew, I knew that it was my mom in crisis.

The nurse told me to go to the consultation room. I got up and went to the door, and as I turned to close it, Brother Kevin came in behind me. How did he know we needed him? I was glad he was there.

I was scared and my thoughts were running wild. Mom needed her family here. What if she died? I would never forgive them for abandoning her.

The doctor came in and said, "Your mother's heartbeat has dropped to thirty beats a minute, and her blood pressure is spiking off the chart. I feel my only option is to take her back to surgery and put in a pacemaker."

There was no guarantee she would survive the surgery. Since I had Power of Attorney, I would have to sign the consent form. If I signed that form and she died, I would never forgive myself. There were no more options and time was running out.

Brother Kevin said, "We must do everything possible to save her life."

I signed the form, and it almost made me sick! Brother Kevin, the doctor, and I held hands and prayed.

How much more could I take? I wanted to scream! Where was God? Why was he letting this happened to her? I needed answers!

Brother Kevin and I went to see mom before they took her to surgery. She was so still. Did she know what was happening? Would she survive?

Brother Kevin got on one side of the bed, and I was on the other side. He held one of her hands, I held one, and we held hands over her body.

He began to pray out loud. The harder he prayed, the louder he got. I looked past the foot of the bed. People were standing outside the glass doors, silent, heads bowed, maybe praying with us. I hoped, God was listening and would help her.

Why would God take a woman who loved him so much? A woman who always put him first, and gave him control of her life.

I've done everything I could. Where are you, God? Save her, I know you can. You can do all things. I believed in my heart that He would not let her die. Her life is in your hands, God, and my faith is in your love and mercy.

At that moment, I realized why we were there. It was to save my life, not to take hers. God brought me there to test my faith. He wanted me to need him for myself, not my mom.

I was the one at death's door. God brought me here alone, to search my soul for the truth. I didn't want to give up control, but the truth was, I never had it.

Forgive me, oh Lord, I know you are my God, thank you for reminding me. I surrendered my life to God, and what ever happened was in his hands. Whatever happens, he will give me the strength to deal with all things.

My mother went to death's door to save my life, not lose hers. I will never forget the gift of forgiveness and a new life because of God's grace.

Brother Kevin and I went back to the waiting room, and mom went to surgery. He said, "I'll stay with you until the surgery is over, and we know that she has come through it."

I told him to go home and be with his family. Mom was in God's hands, and whatever happened was His decision. Brother Kevin hugged my neck and left.

Fifteen minutes later, the phone rang and surgery had started. I sat in my chair and prayed. My mind was clear and my heart was full.

Twenty minutes later, I got the second call. They had entered the heart valve and she was stable. I asked God, for a little while longer with my mom.

The last call came. She was stable and headed to recovery. I whispered, "Thank you, God, Thank you."

Mark came to the waiting room, hugged my neck, and told me to prepare myself for a surprise. When I walked in mom's room, she was sitting up in bed! Her heartbeat and blood pressure were normal!

The pacemaker had saved her life, and God had saved mine. Two miracles in one day! Her face had color, and she spoke of going home. Her recovery would be long, but the worst was over.

My life would be forever changed for the better. I know now that God will go to any lengths to save someone. Looking back, I was supposed to be there alone with only God to turn to.

Telling myself I had faith and proving it was another failure for me. Every time I made a decision without God, I failed. God was reaching out to me, willing to take this burden if I would put my faith and trust in Him.

Though I would never be worthy, He loved me anyway. Every day that I wake up I'm blessed. I will be reminded of God's incredible mercy every time I look into my mother's eyes.

I put her picture back in the bag, covered up and tried

to sleep. The crickets were making noise and the moon was full. I remembered what I said as a child looking out those same windows, on a night like this.

"I see the moon, and the moon sees me. Good night, Frank, I love you."

Chapter 10
Frank

Sunlight coming through the window woke me up. I looked and Frank was still asleep on the couch. I got up and walked out on the porch. Usually, Frank followed me anytime I went outside, but this time he didn't.

I went back in the house, leaned down and kissed him on his head. He didn't move. I rubbed down his back and his skin was cold.

Oh my God, Oh my God, not Frank, not now! My precious Frank was dead. My heart was broke. I picked him up and held him in my arms. I cried until I got sick.

All I said was, "I love you, I love you, please don't leave me!" Why now? Why here? I held him close hoping to find a heartbeat, but it was not to be.

I couldn't breathe. I couldn't let him go. I took off his collar and fell to my knees. I couldn't believe he was gone. I tried to compose myself and prepare to bury him.

I went down to one of the old sheds and found a shovel. I needed to find the perfect place to bury him.

It took most of the day to dig his grave. Frank had been my dearest friend for many years. The secrets he knew and the good times we had were too many to tell.

I went back to the house, wrapped him in his blanket and carried him to his grave. Unprepared for his death, I spoke these words.

You will never be forgotten, and I will love you till I die.

I'd love a few more days, to have you by my side.
To kiss your head, and take you on a ride.
My heart will never mend, but then I'm on my way.
I'll meet you in Heaven, we'll start a brand new day.

I dug Frank's grave beside my grandmother's rose bushes. I held him in my arms, not wanting to let him go. I forced myself to lay him in his grave. With every shovel of dirt, I said, "I love you."

How could I walk away and leave him there all alone? I didn't know how, only that I had to. I told him that he was safe there, and soon the day would come when I would be by his side again.

I went back to the porch, and wept uncontrollably. I was all alone and too upset to leave. It was getting dark so I went inside. I was thankful that Frank didn't suffer, maybe God would show me the same mercy.

I curled up on the couch, where he last slept, but sleep wouldn't come. I held his collar close to my heart. I wanted and needed to remember him. I couldn't let my thoughts of him go.

Tears filled my eyes as memories of him flooded my mind.

I adopted Frank from the Humane Society, where I was a member. He had been there a while, and no one wanted to take him. I never wanted another dog after Sippi died. The heartbreak was too much.

The female dogs and their puppies were filling up the pound and there was little room for other animals. If they weren't adopted in a period of time, they were put down. The pound was very small.

I got a call on Saturday afternoon, and if I couldn't take him, he would be put down on Monday. The thought of this dog dying because no one wanted him haunted my mind.

He had been whipped, shot and left to die. I told them to bring him to my house. Since that day, I never regretted that decision.

I will never know what he suffered on his journey to finding me, but that part of his life was over. I loved and cherished Frank, every day. I am a better person because of him.

Too many memories and reliving them broke my heart. I cried myself to sleep. I awoke the next morning and walked out to Frank's grave. I knelt down and told him I loved him. I thanked Frank for loving me and bringing me years of happiness.

I went back to the house, got our things and loaded the car. I backed down the driveway, and as I passed his grave I blew him a kiss.

I was all alone now and going home to die. The drive home was lonesome. I pulled in the driveway, raised the garage door and prepared to unload my car. I opened the kitchen door and put all my luggage in the dining room.

I walked through the house and everything looked ok. On my way back to the kitchen, I stopped in the dining room and put Frank's collar in the tattered bag.

I called my family, told them I was home and invited them for supper that next evening. My pain was worse. I was very sick. Tomorrow would bring many questions, and I was too tired to answer them.

I decided to write a letter to my family, in the event that I couldn't find the courage to tell them face to face. I took a warm bath and searched for the words to express my thoughts.

I climbed in bed with paper and pen knowing that this would be one of the hardest things I've ever had to do. Burying Frank was the only thing that compared to this.

A few hours later the letter was finished. I put it in a envelope, sealed it and addressed it to my family with love. Tears ran down my face, as I prayed for the courage to tear the letter up, but I couldn't.

I felt nauseous. I needed a drink of water. I started to the kitchen, and as I walked through the dining room, I laid the letter on the table. I reached in the cabinet for a glass and everything went dark. I felt myself falling.

Chapter 11
The Letter

"I'm cold," she thought, but couldn't move. "I need help"

She was slipping in and out of consciousness, and her thoughts were scattered. Light began to fill the room. Night had turned to day.

She remembered that her family was coming for dinner. "If I can just hold on they'll find me," she whispered.

"Knocking, I hear knocking, Help me!" she spoke trying to cry out, and then the knocking stopped.

She closed her eyes and prayed. When she opened them again, Andrew was kneeling over her screaming for his mother.

"Oh my God, call nine, one, one Mom. Mamma is on the kitchen floor, something is wrong! See if she's breathing, Luke!"

"She's alive," Luke yelled. "Call an ambulance!"

"I am, I am," their mother responded. "There's nothing cooking on the stove, what's going on!"

Her daughter knelt down beside her on the floor. She was very thin and pale. Something was wrong, very wrong. What was she keeping from us? How long had she been on the floor?

The ambulance finally got there. They put her on a stretcher, and we followed in our car. It seemed like forever until we got to the hospital.

Doctors began to work on my mother and bombard me with questions. Questions I couldn't answer. We sat in the waiting room wondering how this happened.

Luke asked, "What about Frank?" They didn't

remember seeing or hearing him at mamma's house. What was going on? The boys decided to go back to mom's house and look for him.

"We'll call when we find him," Andrew said. They pulled in the garage, expecting to hear Frank bark, but there was no sound.

Luke unlocked the door and went inside. He called and called Frank, but he never came. Andrew was checking out the backyard, but he wasn't there either.

"Mamma's going to be upset if we don't find him," Luke said. "Let's go next door to Ms. Vera's and ask for her help."

Ms. Vera was mamma's favorite neighbor. A southern speaking lady that made a mean pan of fudge. There was a gate in the fence between them. This was their pathway to one another's yards.

Luke and Andrew found Ms. Vera and told her about Frank and mamma. Ms. Vera told them that she would watch for Frank, and for them to keep her updated on mamma.

They thanked Ms. Vera and went back to the house to lock up, but they checked every room and closet one more time.

"Luke, Luke, hurry, come here," Andrew was screaming.

On the dining room table was a letter that read, "To My Family With Love." Tear stains had smudged the word, Love. Andrew picked it up, locked the door, and they went back to the hospital.

"Wonder what it says," Luke asked. "Should we open it? We better wait and let mom open it."

When they got to the waiting room, a doctor was asking their mother questions. They sat down and listened.

"Who is her doctor?" the man asked.

"She has two doctors, a Cardiologist, and her family doctor," her daughter replied.

"Who is her Oncologist?" he asked again.

"She doesn't have cancer, what are you talking about?" her daughter replied sternly!

"Our tests show her cancer is in the final stage, and this strain has no cure." the man said with certainty.

I grasped my heart. It can't be. She never told us. What the hell was going on! They were moving her to Intensive Care. She was going in and out of consciousness, but they let me see her for a few minutes.

I walked into her room. Her eyes were closed, and I sensed death. This wasn't the woman I had seen a month ago.

I touched her hand and said, "I'm here, mom, I'm here."

I went back to the waiting room. What would I tell Andrew and Luke? Within minutes, mom went into a coma.

The doctor said, "You need to call the family and her pastor." I stood there in shock! What was going on? I called Brother Jimmy, and he was on his way.

Mom and Frank had just taken a vacation. Did she know she was sick? Why didn't she tell us? I needed these questions answered!

I went back to the waiting room to tell the boys as much as I knew, which was very little. When I saw them, they were in a panic! They didn't find Frank, but they found a letter.

Andrew handed it to me, and I began to weep. It's true, she knew all the time. The boys had no idea what was going on.

Luke asked, "What's wrong, mom?"

“Mamma’s been sick for a long time, and I don’t know why she didn’t tell us.”

The doctor came and took us to her room. She was getting worse. It was a matter of time, now. Brother Jimmy came in the room, and we all held hands and prayed.

Brother Jimmy told us that he didn’t know mom was sick. I told him neither did we. I handed him the letter. I asked him to open it and read it.

To My Family With Love.

To ask yourselves why, is a waste of time. I chose not to tell anyone that I was dying. I wanted my family to remember me as I was, not consumed by this disease. I never wanted you to count minutes until I died.

Remember every day, not just the special ones. Who was I in your eyes? I hope the best I could’ve been. I can’t say I love you, enough. My life would have been worthless without you.

I believe that God sent me on that journey, not just to look back, but to go forward. If I learned anything, it’s that I truly knew nothing. I would love to go back, but I can’t. I wanted to die with no regrets, but time didn’t allow.

Though my tears were many, my blessings were more. Yesterday filled me with regrets, today reminds me that tomorrow never comes and isn’t promised.

I asked myself what it meant to have it all? For me, the answer was peace. Being at peace with every decision, or not making it until I was.

Don’t look for Frank, he died in his sleep at my old home place, and I buried him beside my grandmother’s rose bushes.

Make your own paths, don’t follow in anyone’s

footsteps. Your life was written for you. Leave your own mark in this world.

A child has no worries, a young person thinks they know it all, and older people await death and are thankful for every day.

Laugh or smile when you think of me. I had it all and then some. The good days outweighed the bad. My life was a miracle and so is yours.

I am leaving one part of my family, to join another. I'll be watching over all of you, somewhere, somehow. I Love You

My Wishes

I don't want a public funeral or memorial service. I want to be buried in the Red Hill Cemetery with the rest of my family. After you read my request, I want you to go to my house, open a bottle of my finest wine, get out the old tattered bag and open it.

What happens next, I hope and pray will give you the answers you're looking for.

Brother Jimmy folded the pages and gave them back to me. We gathered around her bed and prayed. She opened her eyes, for just a moment, whispered, "I love you," then she died.

Disbelief and heartbreak filled the room. How could this be? Was she really dead? Why was this trip so important?

It was apparent she didn't want to discuss her illness, or burden her family. What would life be like without Mom or Frank.

We went back to mom's house to honor her wishes. We pulled in the driveway, the house was dark, and Frank didn't greet us with a bark.

"My God, My God, how could this be?" I whispered with a broken heart. Andrew opened the kitchen door and turned on the lights. Mom's luggage was still in the dining room.

"What do I do now?" I screamed. "I wasn't prepared for this!"

Luke said, "Mamma's letter told us what to do."

Get the old tattered bag, boys, and I'll get her finest bottle of wine. I was reminded of how she served wine on special occasions.

I poured me a glass of wine, and poured two glasses of soda for the boys. We went into the living room, formed a circle on the floor around the tattered bag and for a moment, sat there in silence.

The boys were ready for me to open the bag. The tattered bag was worn and frayed. It's zipper only closed half-way. It had taken its last journey. Mom never traveled without it.

What would be inside and why was it important for us to open it now. The boys wanted me to go first.

****

I unzipped the bag and reached inside. I pulled out Frank's collar and began to cry. Mom loved him so much. I bet she felt then, what I feel now, having to bury someone that you love.

I always complained every time Frank licked me. I can't stand a dog to lick on me! I always told him no, and pushed him away. He only wanted to show me his love. I'm sorry Frank. I read every tag on his collar, one for every year of his life.

Andrew went next. He reached in and pulled out his baseball cap. He covered his face to hide his emotions, but his tears were visible. He held it up and saw the writing inside.

He said, "Mamma wrote something inside!"

Luke yelled, "Read it, Read it!"

It said, Stayin alive with 25. Oh my God, Mamma remembered that game.

"What game, what does it mean?" Luke asked.

Luke was a little boy when Andrew played that game and didn't remember, so Andrew relived the game, play by play for Luke. Tears were beginning to turn to laughter.

****

Luke went last. He reached in the bag and pulled out the red coin purse.

Luke said, "Mamma kept her cuss money in here and it's full!" He poured out the coins and touched them all. With a smile on his face, he looked at Andrew and said, "This time, you get all the nickels!" We laughed out loud at Luke's revenge.

****

We continued to pull out pieces and relive their place in our lives until the tattered bag was empty. Some things we pulled out we knew nothing about. Those were her personal memories.

The tattered bag had revealed a peace that was hoped for. How humble it made us feel to know that, we were what she chose to remember on her journey to death.

We put everything back in the bag and just looked at each other.

Andrew said, "Let's toast Mamma, we'll each make a toast!"

****

Andrew said, "You never put yourself first, and you made sure that I was never last. I Love You."

"My turn," Luke said. "You saw me take my first breath, and I saw you take your last. I only wish I could have held you in my arms like you held me in yours. I'll always be your Chuga Bear."

It was my turn, and I said, "I'm not ready to say good-bye, and I can't thank you enough. I make you this promise. We will cherish the tattered bag, add new memories to it, and relive them often. I will always remember how blessed I was to know and love one of God's greatest miracles, you. My prayer is that you are in Heaven with the man you loved so much, your grandfather, Sippi and Frank. Thank you for the Tattered bag.

The End.

Bio

Born and raised in Mississippi, Margaret Eubanks still resides there today with her adopted dog, Frank.

She is the author of four books, available in paperback and on Kindle –

Whispers

Good Night, Sippi, I Love You

Ankepi: The Keeper of the Angel Wall

The Tattered Bag: A Life Remembered.

Made in the USA
Columbia, SC
31 July 2023

21092812R00041